EASTER
DOT TO DOT

DOD & COLOR

EASTER BASKET STUFFERS

HAPPY Easter

Thank you for purchasing our book. Our team has worked hard to create this book and we kindly ask for your <u>feedback.</u>

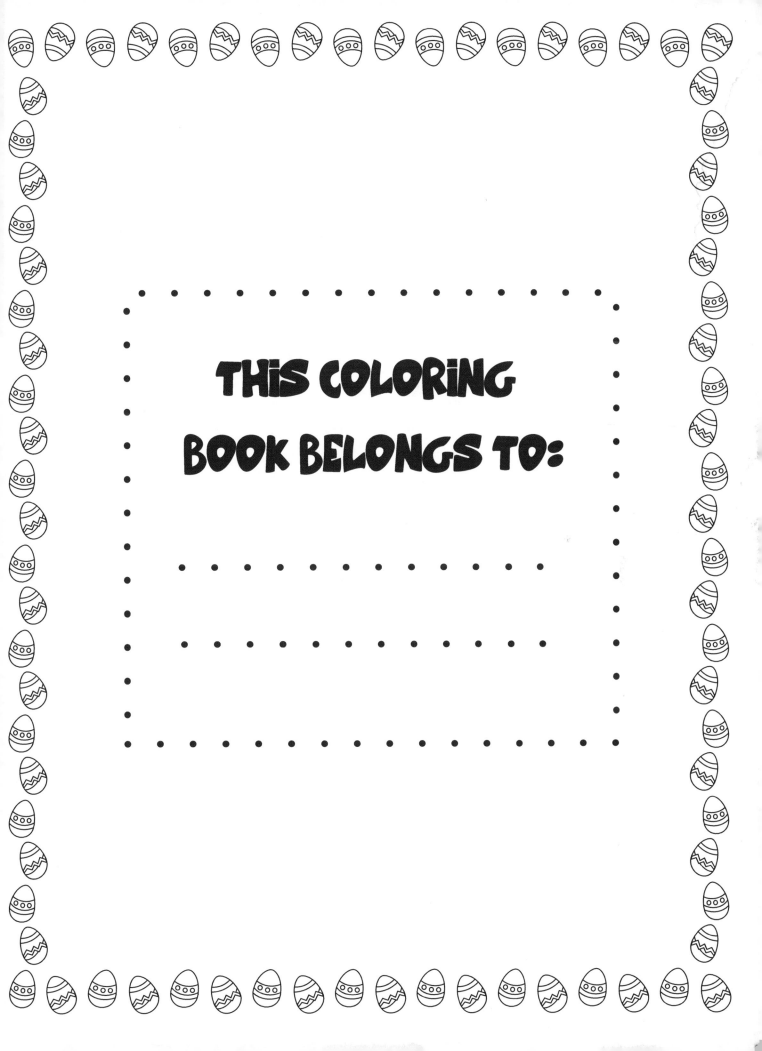

THIS COLORING BOOK BELONGS TO:

TEST COLOR

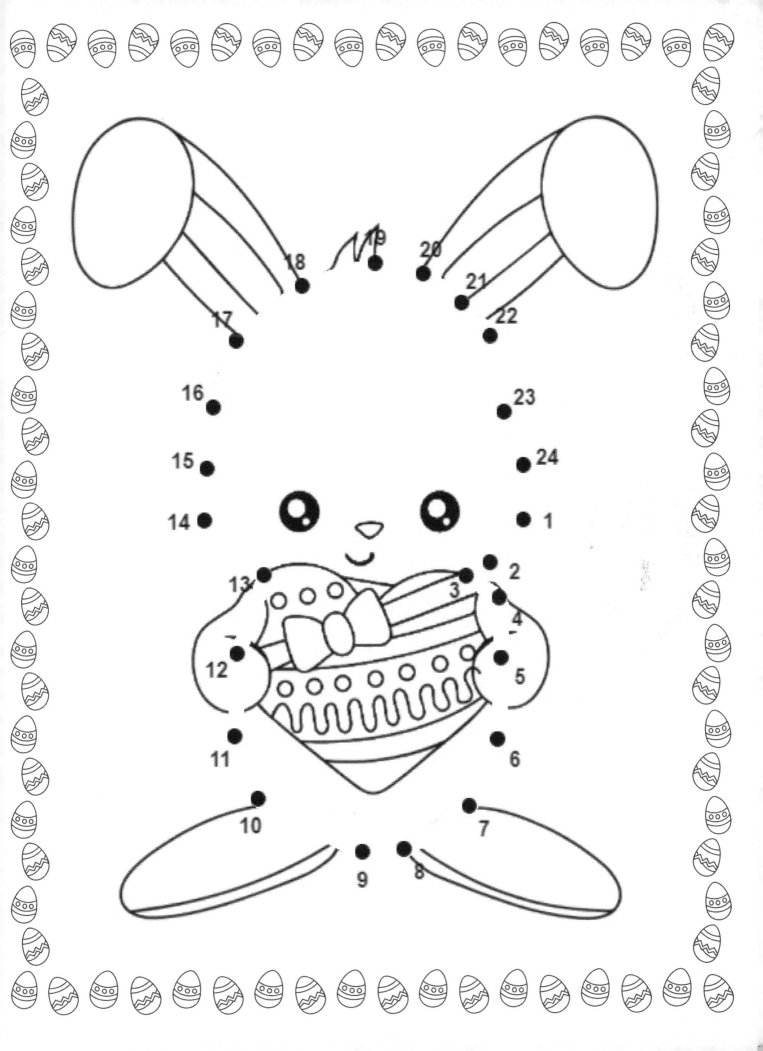

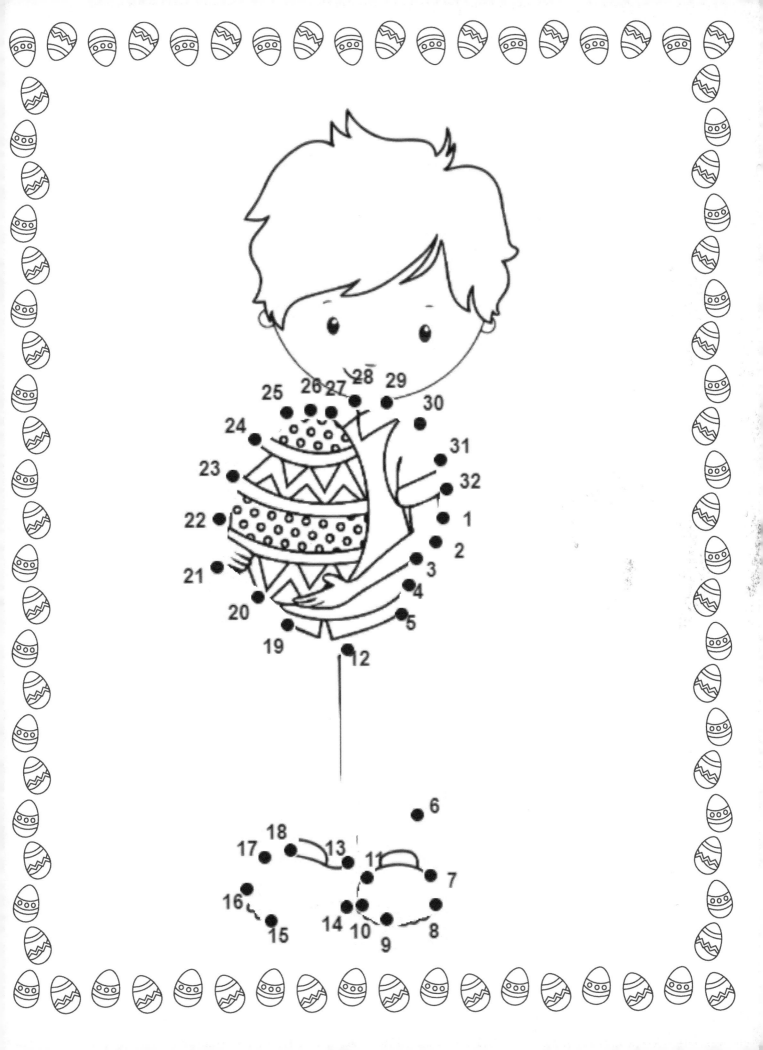

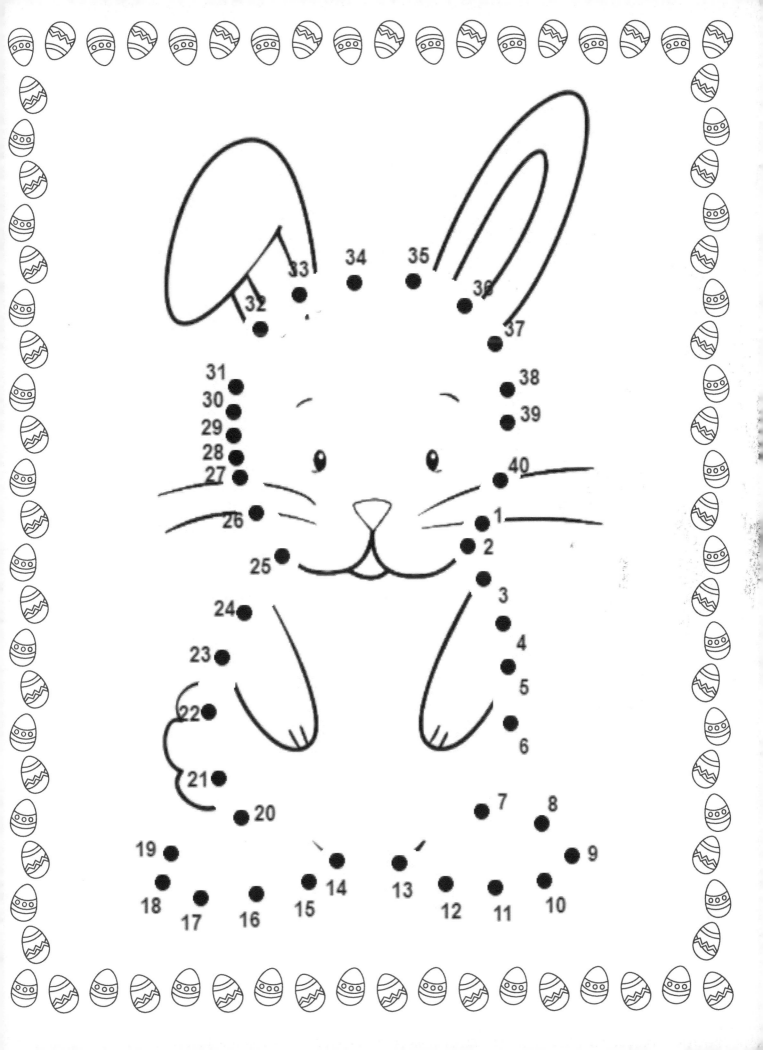

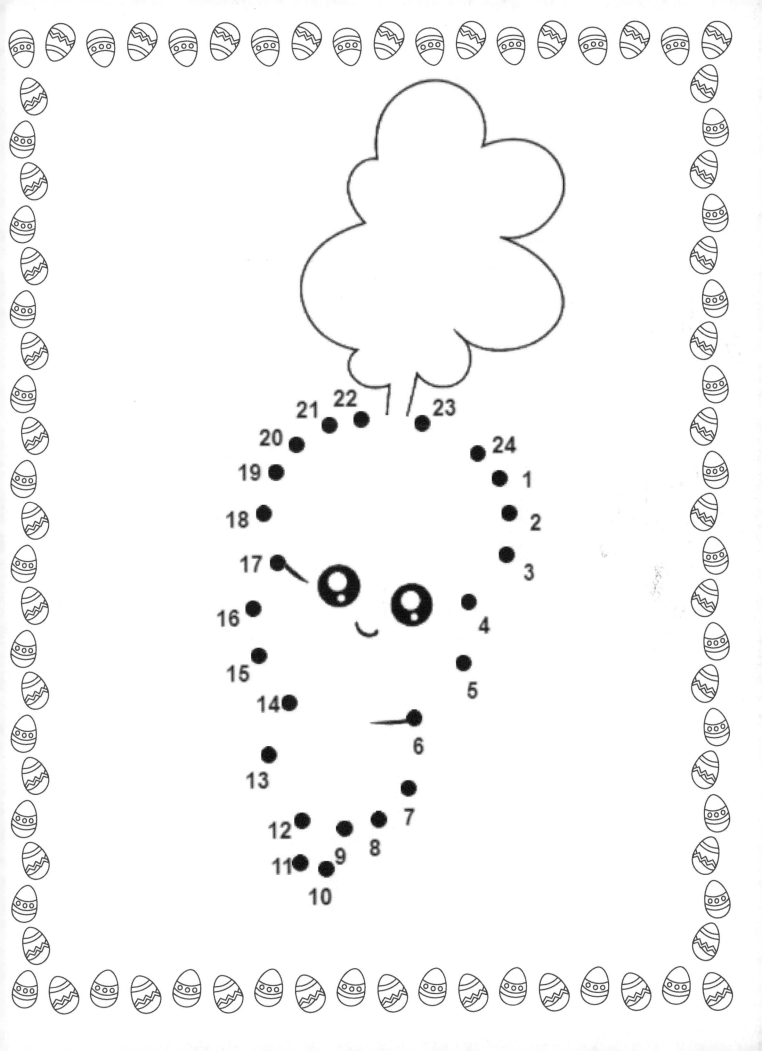

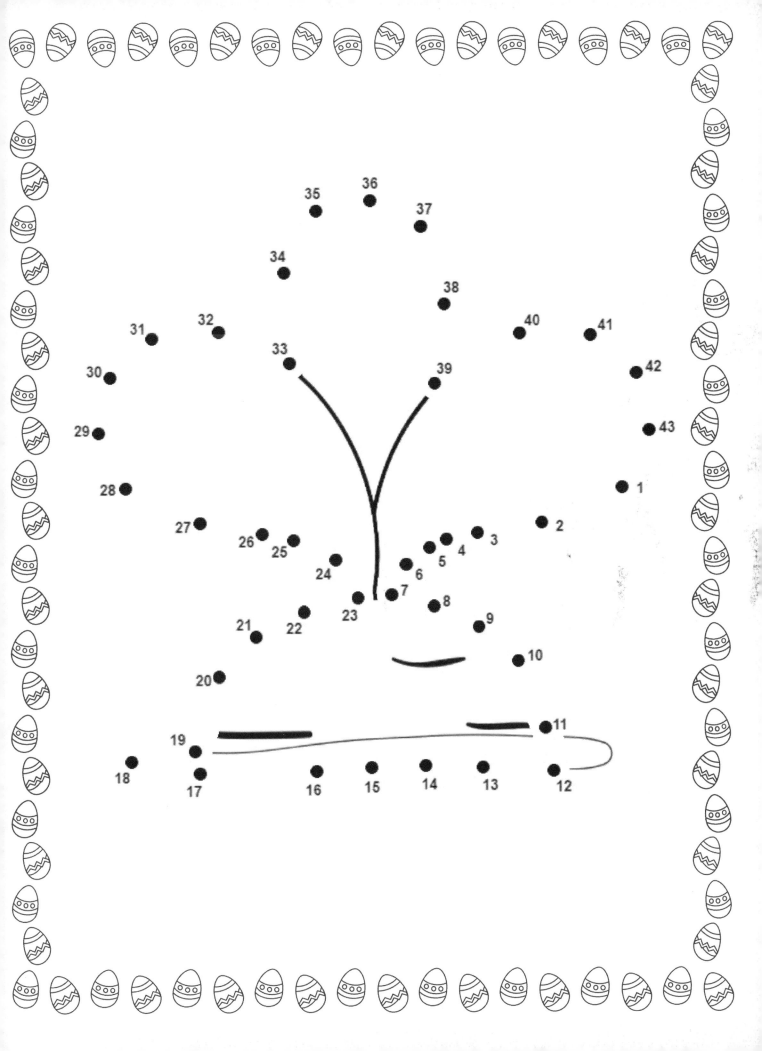

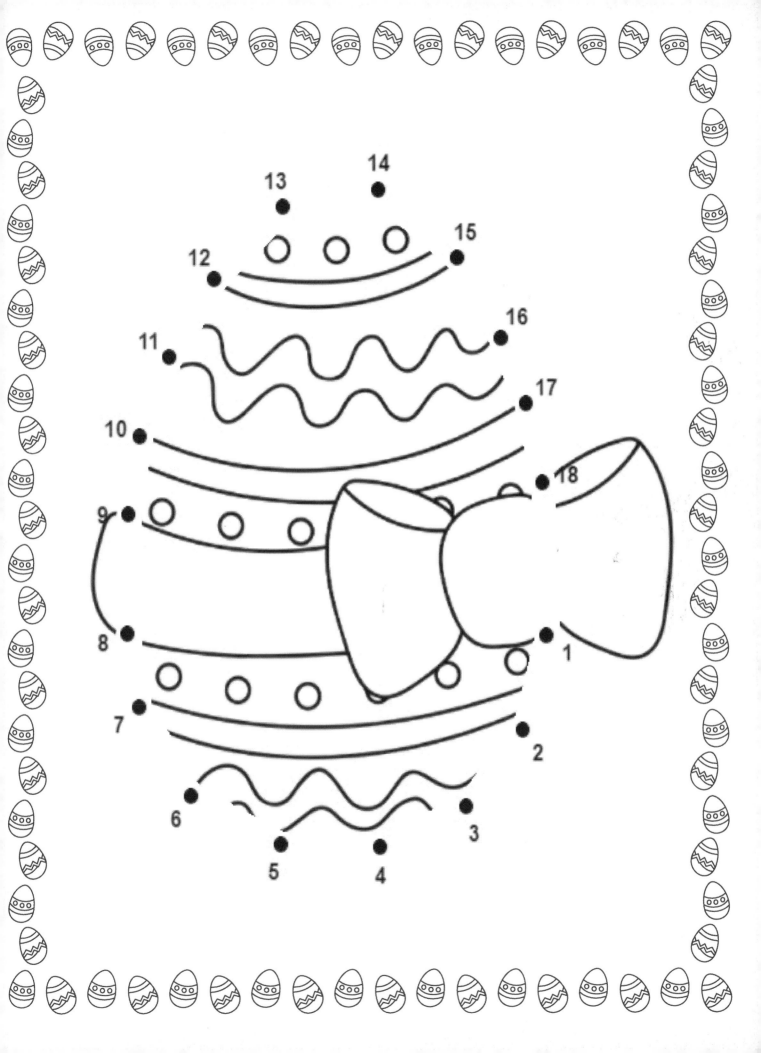

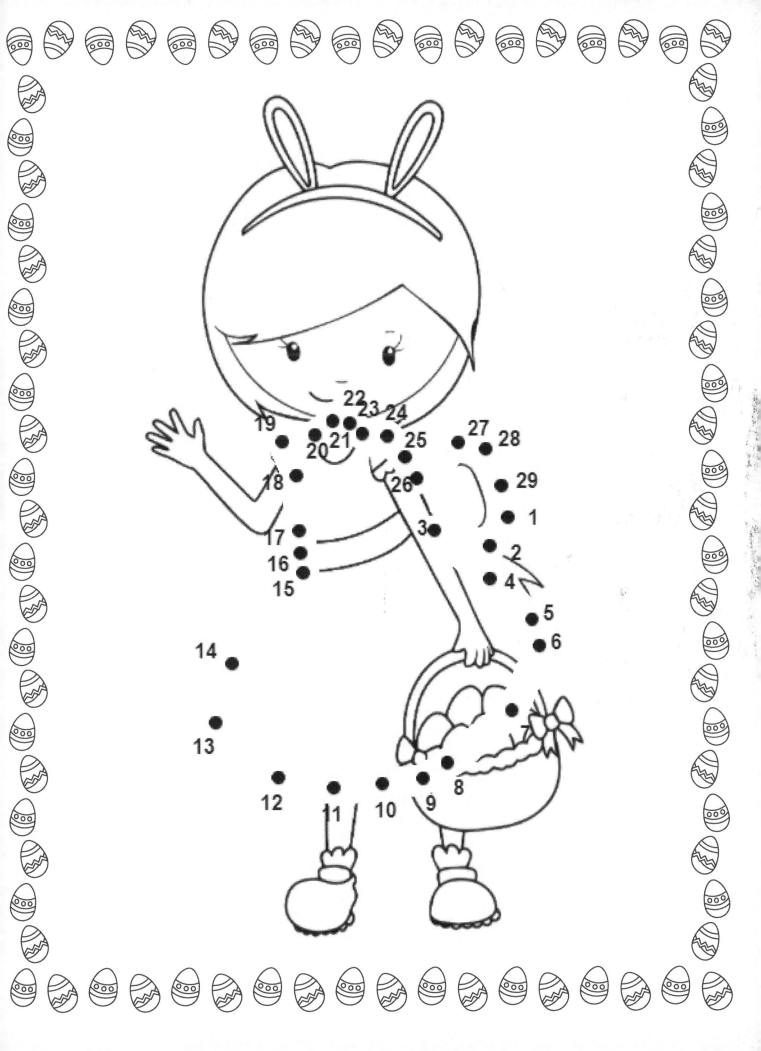

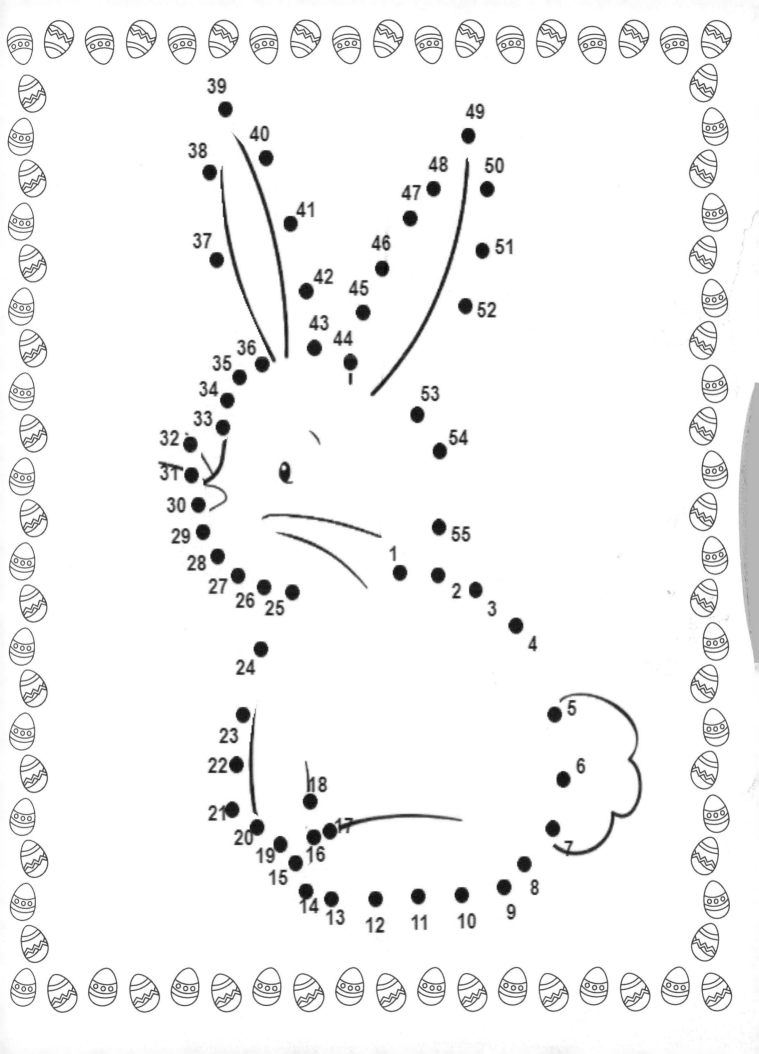

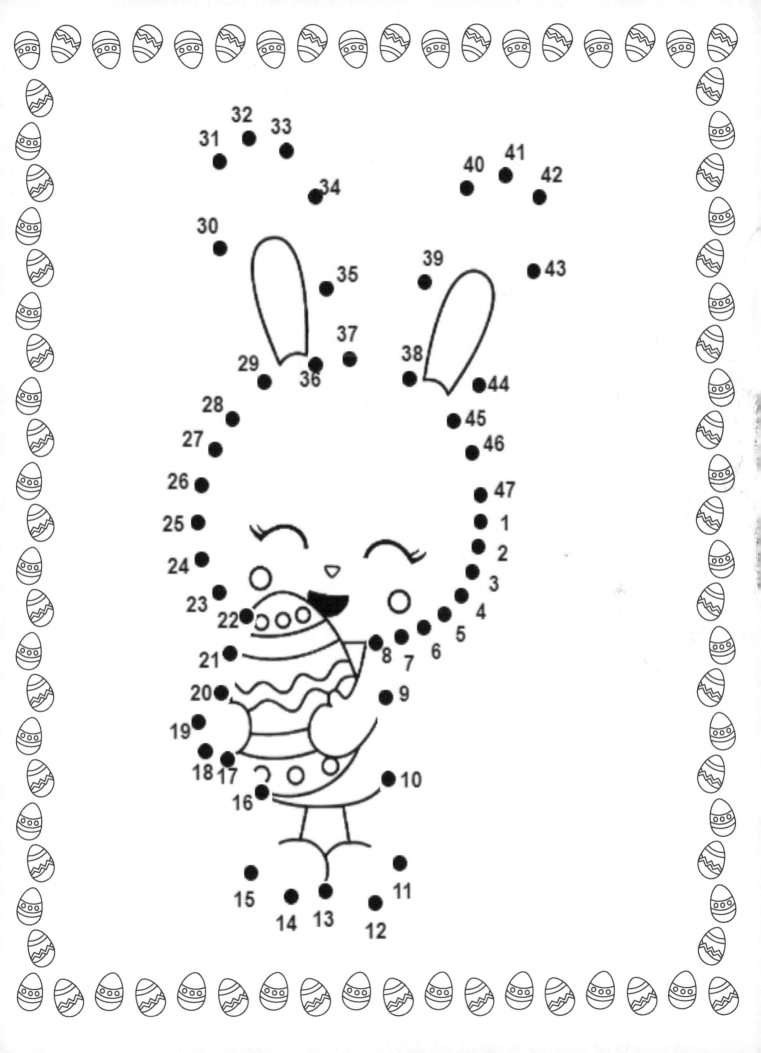

HAPPY Easter

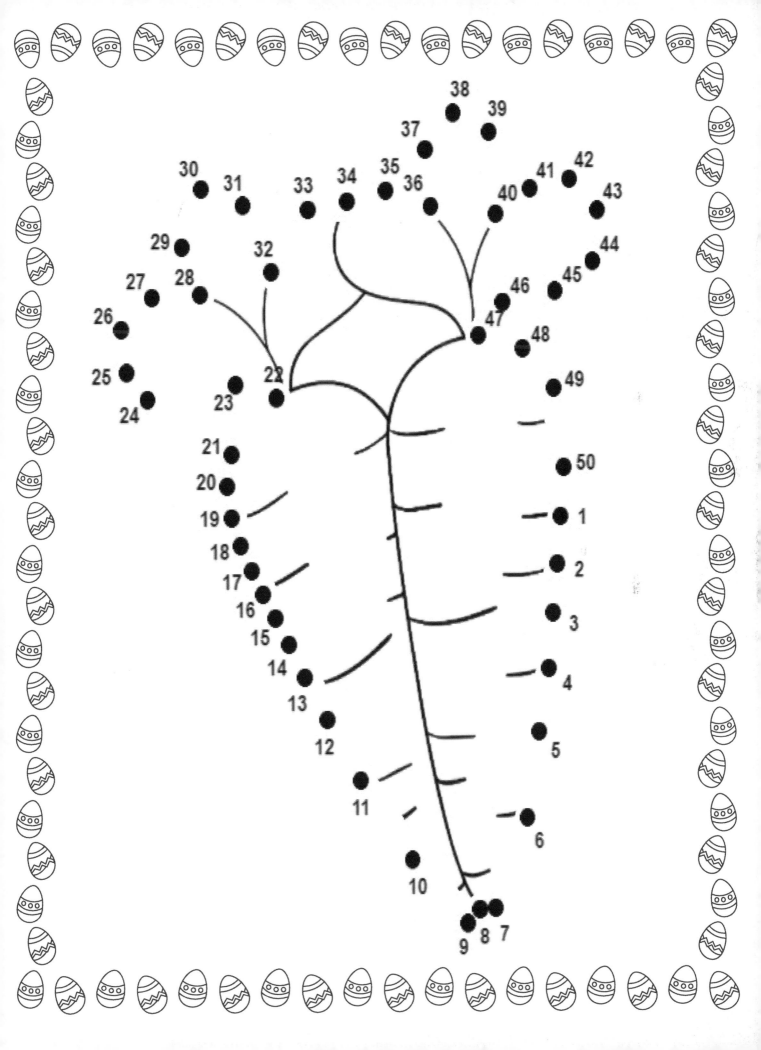

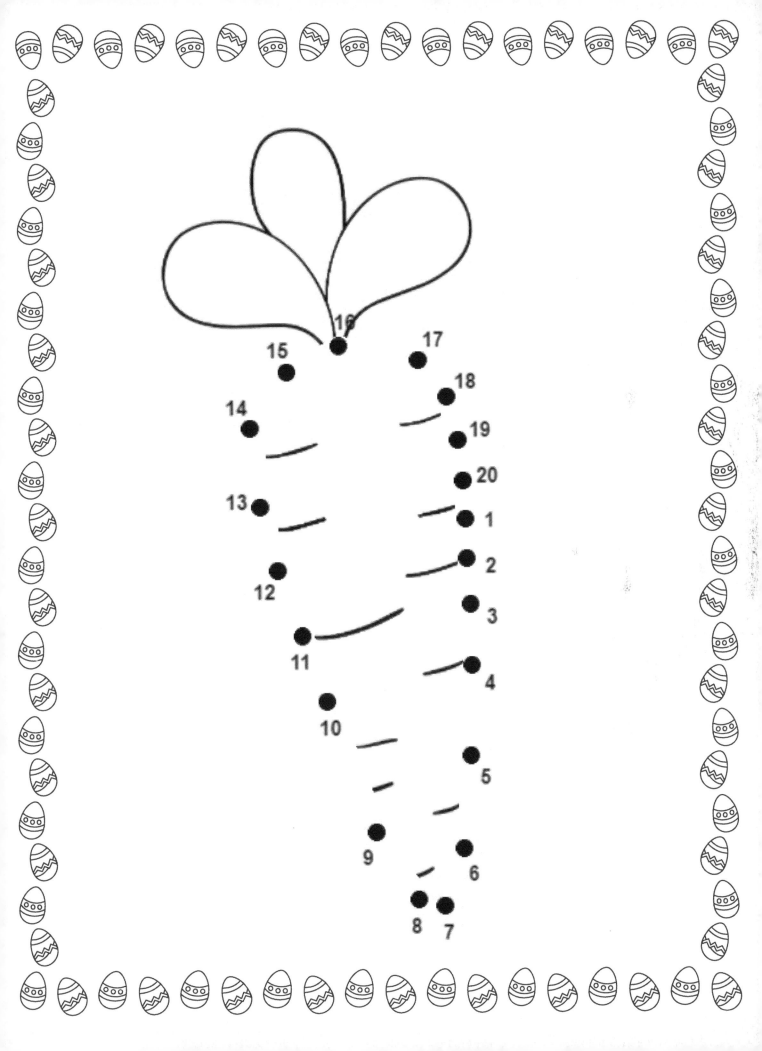

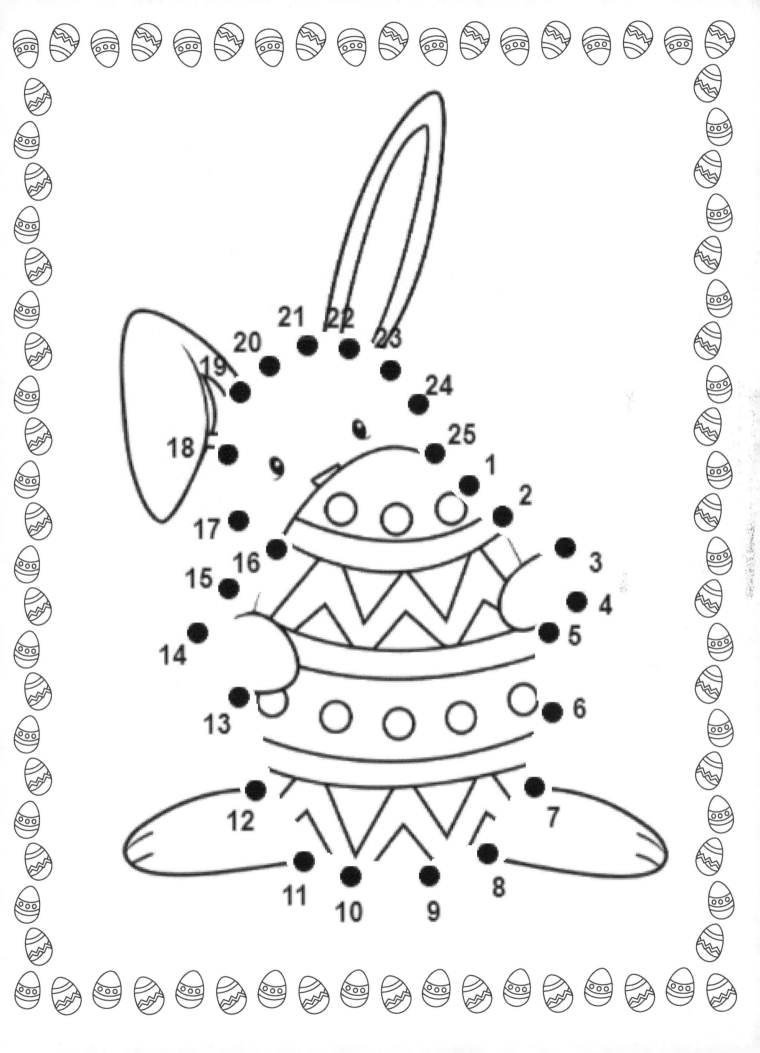

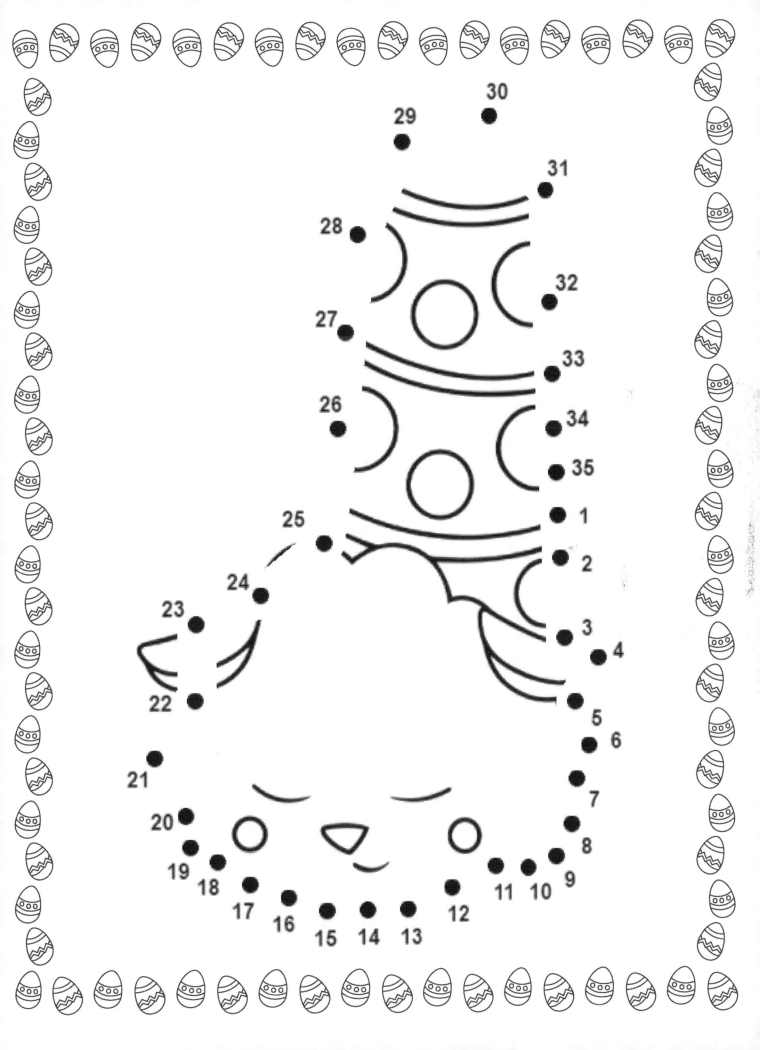

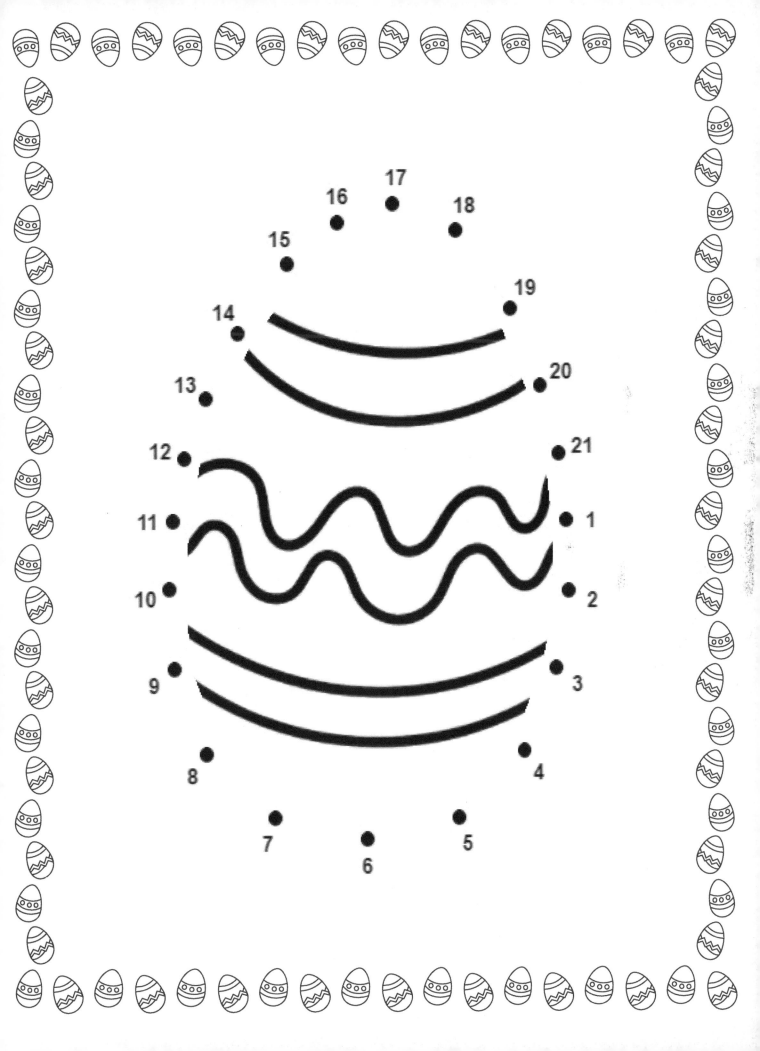

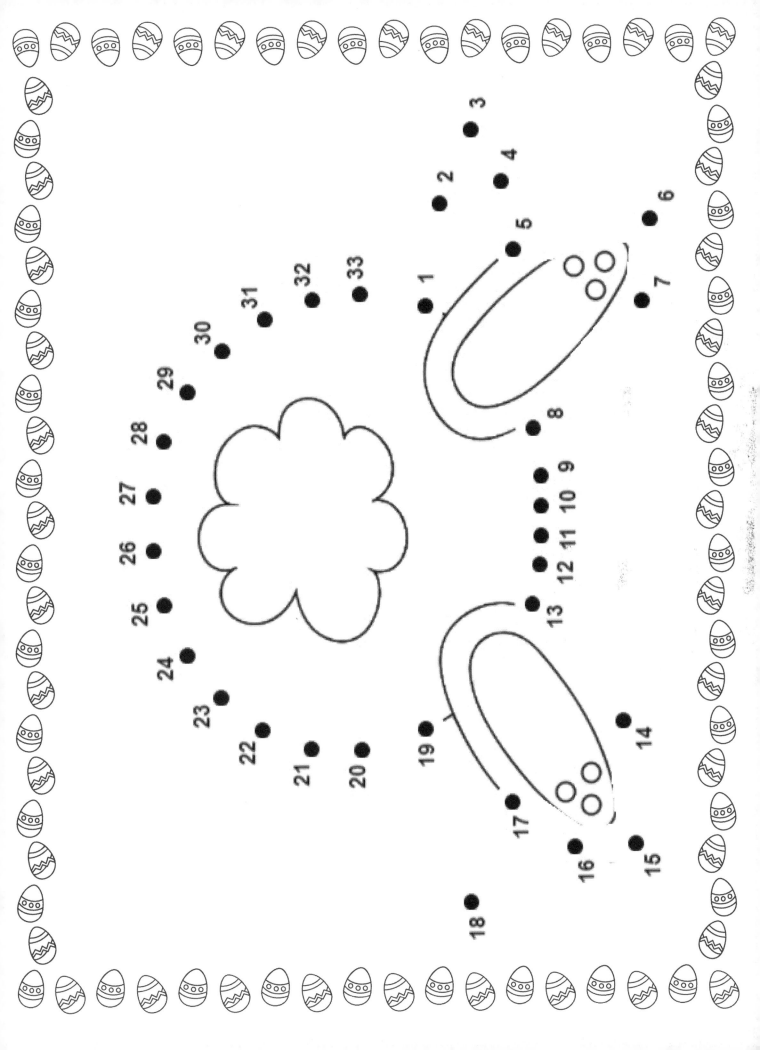

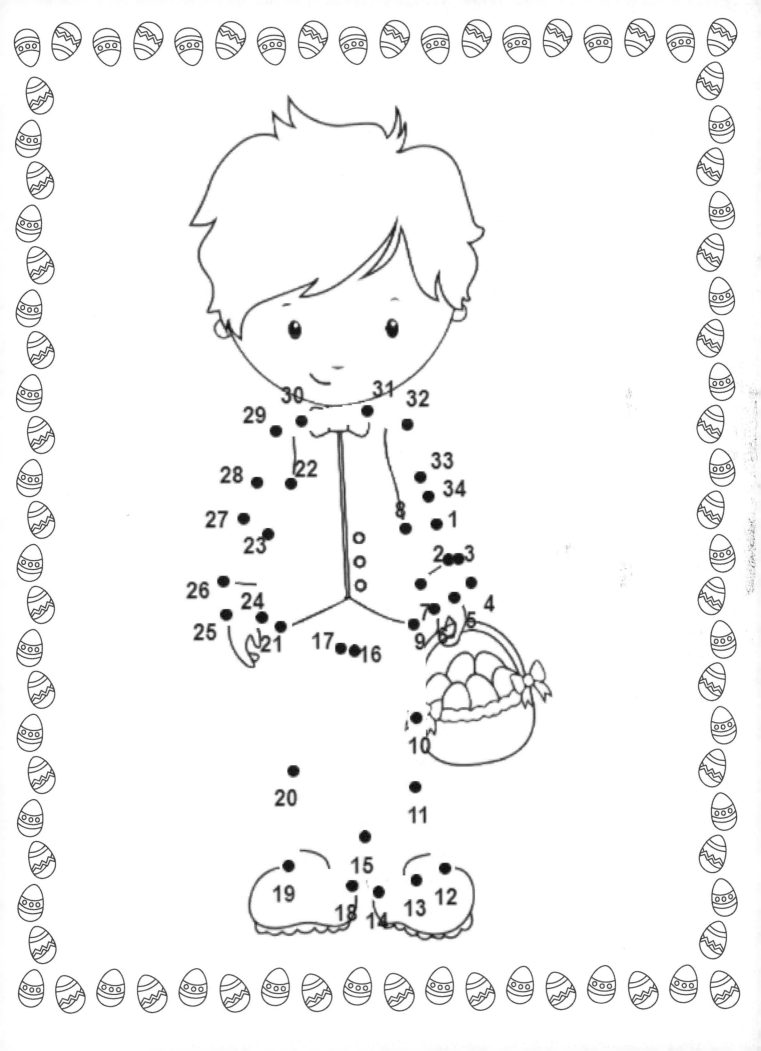

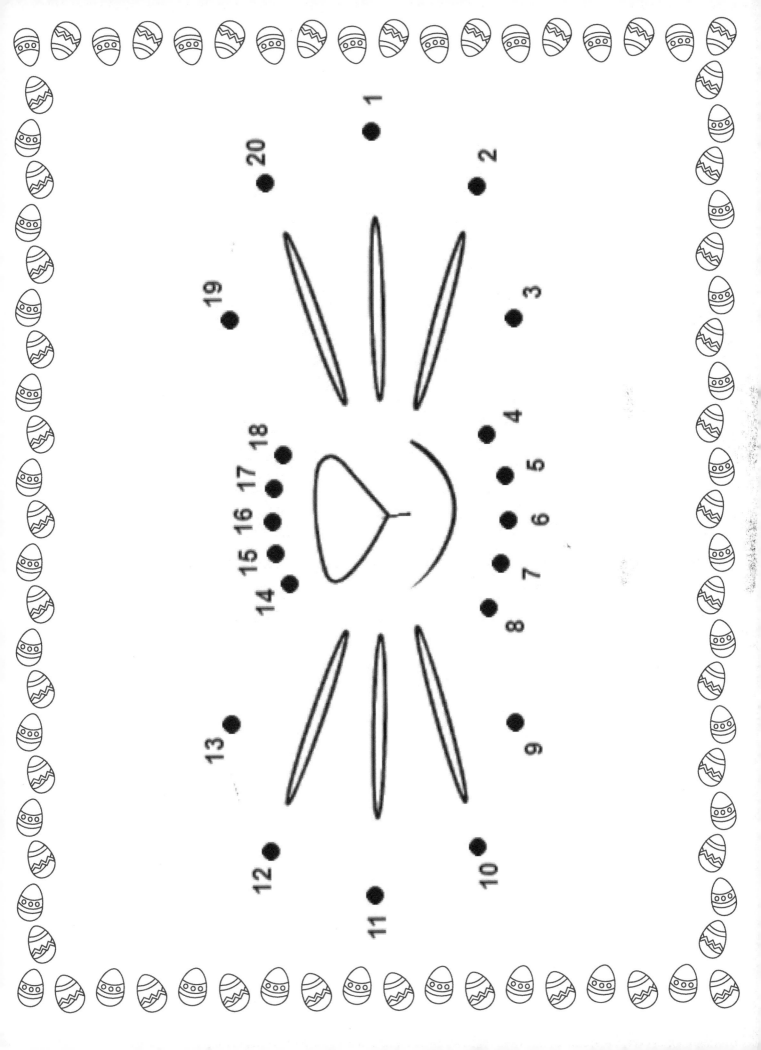

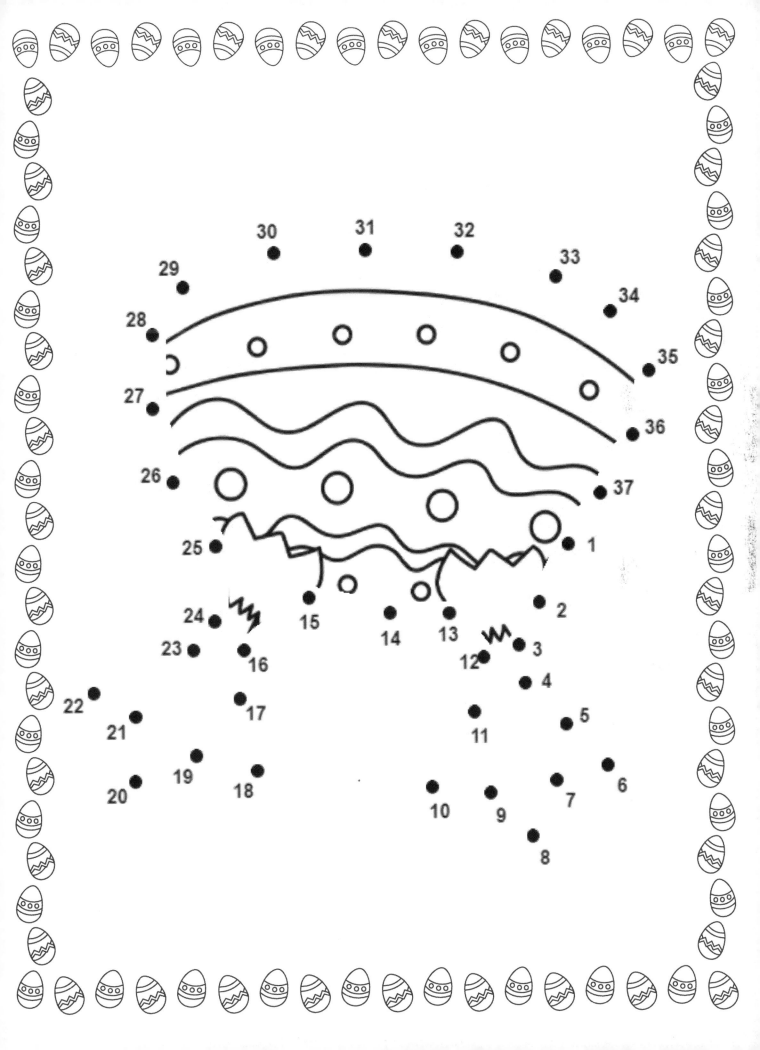

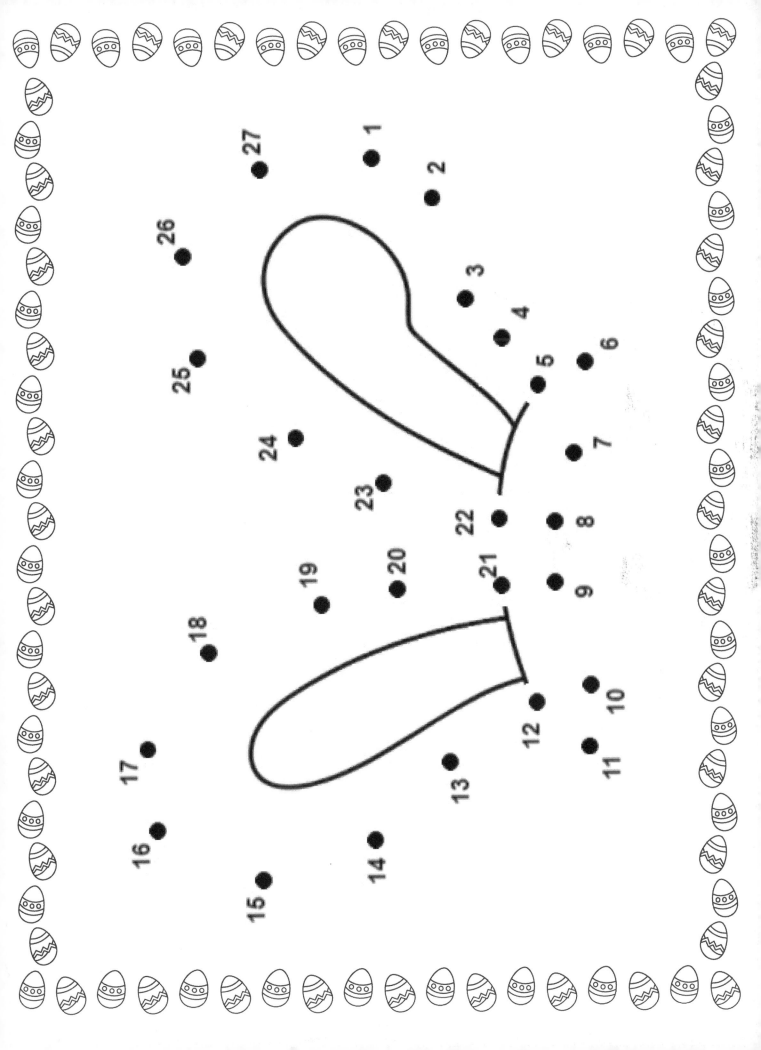

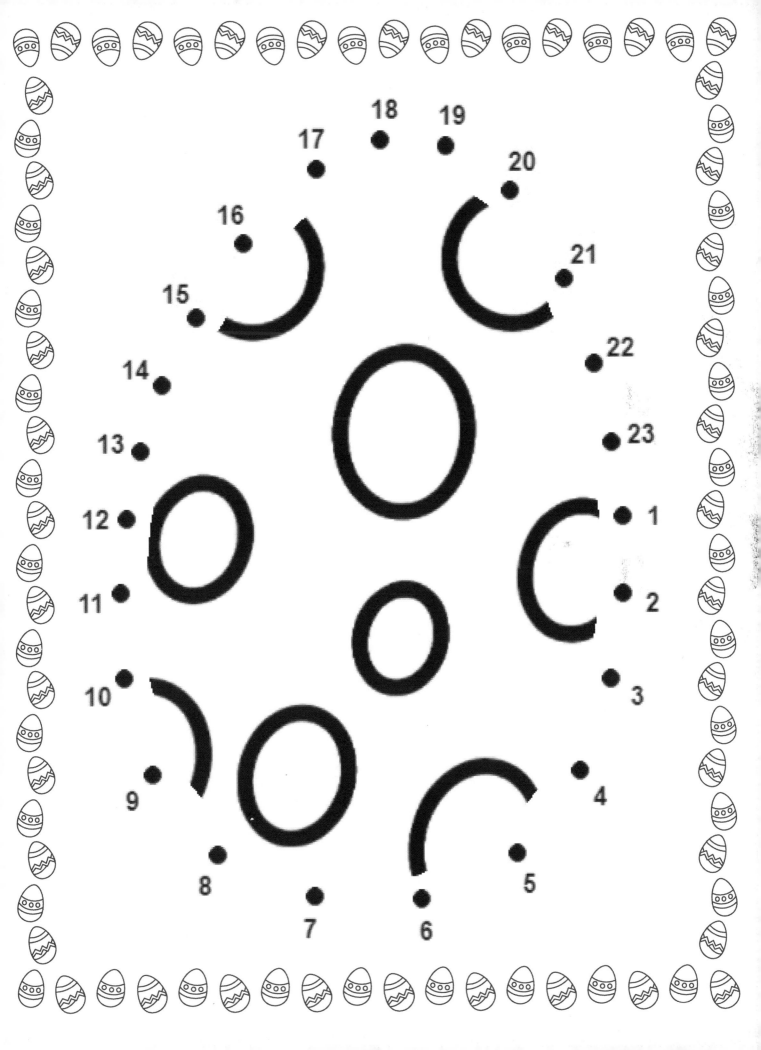

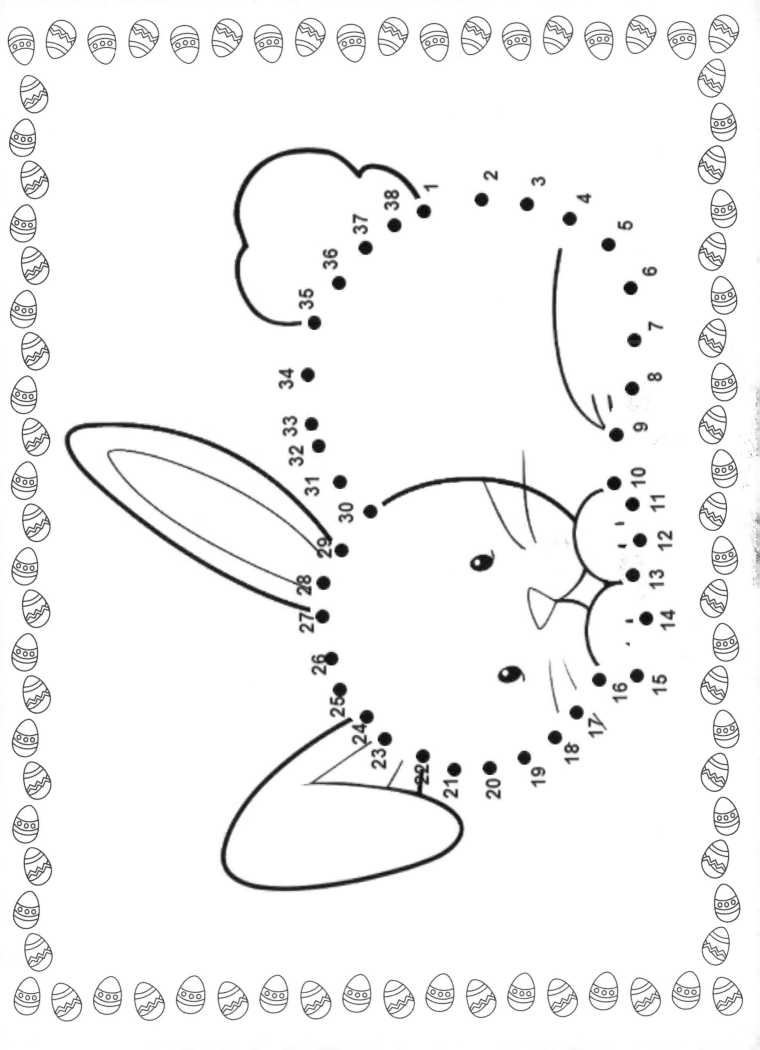

WE ARE PREPARED SPECIAL SUPRISE FOR YOU!

IT'S AN EASTER ACTIVITY EBOOK ABSOLUTELY FOR FREE

SAMPLE PAGES OF EBOOK

THE EBOOK IS COLORFUL!

SCAN THIS QR CODE TO GET IT

DON'T WAIT GET YOUR EBOOK NOW!

Made in the USA
Coppell, TX
30 March 2023

14964252R00052